# The Baobab
# that Opened Its Heart

*and*

*Other Nature Tales for Children*

LAITMAN
KABBALAH PUBLISHERS

**The Baobab that Opened Its Heart
and Other Nature Tales for Children**

Copyright © 2010 by MICHAEL LAITMAN

Published by Laitman Kabbalah Publishers
www.kabbalah.info
info@kabbalah.info

1057 Steeles Avenue West, Suite 532,
Toronto, ON, M2R 3X1,
Canada

Bnei Baruch USA,
2009 85th street, #51,
Brooklyn, NY 11214,
USA

Printed in Canada

ISBN 978-1-897448-53-3
Authors:
Crystlle Medansky,
Shoshana Glizerina,
Lydia Hora,
Meira Levi,
Debbie Sirt,
Marina Fateeva

Copy Editor: Claire Gerus
Illustrations: Sigute Sidabre
Layout and Cover Design: Elinor Twena, Baruch Khovov
Printing and Post Production: Uri Laitman
Executive Editor: Chaim Ratz

FIRST EDITION: SEPTEMBER 2011
First printing

# CONTENTS

# One Song

*By Crystlle Medansky*

Far away in the deep blue ocean, there lived a little humpback whale named Finley. It was his first year migrating across the ocean with the rest of the humpback pod. Finley was very excited. He could hardly wait to get to the warm tropical waters.

"How much farther?" he asked. "Are we there yet?"

"Slow down, Finley," his mother replied. "Sometimes when you are looking for things that are out of reach, you miss the things that are right in front of you."

Now Finley did look around as he swam. And everywhere he looked, he saw bright fish sparkling and leaping out of the water. This made Finley so excited that he felt as if he would burst. He swam quickly around the pod of humpbacks toward the fish.

Suddenly, a fishing net drifting in the water caught him. He tried swimming out of the net. He tried leaping out of the net. He tried diving out of the net. Finally, Finley became so tangled in the net that he could not move at all.

"Help!" moaned Finley, but he had swum too far away from the pod and the others did not hear him.

"Maybe they can still see me!" Finley decided, and began to blow bubbles out of his spout, creating a circle of bubbles around himself.

Soon, a group of seagulls saw the bubbles and dove down to scoop up fish for lunch. That was when they discovered that the little whale was in trouble. Immediately, they forgot all about lunch.

"Hold the net! Hold the net!" they squawked to one another.

The seagulls tried to hold the net afloat with their webbed feet. But although Finley was just a little whale, he was really not so little, and the net began to sink under his weight.

Alarmed, the seagulls began to screech and squawk for help.

Sebastian the sailfish was basking nearby admiring his beautiful blue sail fin when he heard the commotion.

"Bother, why are you making such a noise!" he demanded, swimming over. "Can't you see I am sunning my fin here?"

"Help! Help!" screeched the seagulls. "The little whale is drowning in the net!"

When Sebastian realized that Finley was trapped, he immediately stopped thinking of himself and quickly cut through the net with his big sharp spear to free the little humpback.

"Hooray!" shouted the seagulls.

"Thank you, my friends! You saved my life!" said Finley. "I would like so very much to stay and play with you, but I need to hurry back to the pod. We are traveling to warm waters today."

"Of course, and have a safe journey!" the friends replied.

Finley looked in every direction, but he did not see the humpbacks. He sang out to them, but the pod was too far away to hear.

"Oh, no!" moaned Finley. "I am lost. The pod is too far away to hear my song. How will I ever find them?"

"Don't worry," said Sebastian, "I swim very fast. I will swim quickly to my friends, the dolphins. They will help you find your pod."

When the dolphins realized the little humpback had been separated from his pod, they joined him and began clicking and whistling loudly to help get the other humpbacks' attention. Still, the whales did not hear them, but the Great Blue whale did.

The Great Blue whale is the strongest whale in the ocean. His deep song can travel thousands of miles across the ocean, and he had heard many songs. But these clicking and singing sounds puzzled him, so he decided to unravel the mystery.

"What is this song you are singing?" he asked, swimming over to the group.

"This little whale is lost," clicked the dolphins, "and we are trying to help him find his way home."

The Great Blue whale smiled. "If you teach me your song," he said to Finley, "I will sing this song to all the humpbacks in the ocean and help you find your way home."

Finley quickly taught the Great Blue whale his song. Soon, the little whale's melody echoed so loudly through the ocean that all the fish and animals could hear it.

When the humpbacks heard the song, they quickly realized that Finley was searching for them. Right away, they sang the song back so the lost little whale would know where to find them.

Finley and all his friends were delighted to hear the humpback song returning to them.

"We will swim and fly together with you," announced the Great Blue whale, "just to make sure that you return to your pod safely!"

As the happy friends swam closer and closer to the warm tropical waters, the humpbacks began to hear the most beautiful song: the seagulls were crackling, Sebastian the sailfish was splashing, the dolphins were whistling, and Finley and the Great Blue whale were singing together in harmony.

When the humpbacks heard this beautiful song, they quickly swam out to join the celebration! At last, Finley was home with the humpback pod.

"Thank you all for helping me find my way in the great ocean," said Finley. "I will miss you very much," he added sadly.

"Don't be sad, little one," said the Great Blue whale. "We are all connected like drops of water in the ocean. When you truly love your friends, you are connected forever. Wherever we are in the great world ocean, we are together in one song!"

# A Droplet

*Shoshana Glizerina*

One day, a mother brought her son to the ocean. Together they watched as it gently splashed against the shore.

"Look, this is the mighty ocean," the mother told her son. And a little droplet named Dewy was listening.

"That's interesting! Why did she call the ocean 'mighty'?" Dewy wondered.

"Do you really want to know?" the ocean asked the droplet.

"Yes, I really do!" he replied.

"First you must go on a journey," the ocean said, "and when you return, I will let you know the answer."

The ocean slammed two waves into each other, and Dewy was sent flying up into the sky, shimmering in the sun.

Then, a dark cloud came over the sky and covered the sun.

"Finally!" the cloud said. "We've been waiting for you. Now the journey will begin."

The cloud called out to the wind, and the wind carried the cloud on her shoulders farther and farther from the ocean. It wasn't easy for the strong

wind to carry such a big, heavy cloud, but she carried it along until a loud burst of thunder sounded across the sky.

"Here the fields of wheat need water," the cloud boomed. Until then it had not spilled a single drop. Relieved, the wind immediately stopped and Dewy rushed toward the ground.

***

While falling to the ground, the droplet was in such a hurry that he ran ahead of his friends.

"I need to return to the ocean so he can tell me why he is called 'mighty,'" Dewy said.

Then, suddenly, a stalk of wheat spoke to him: "Droplet, would you quench my thirst, please?"

"I am in a hurry," Dewy replied, "but if you need my help, I will stay," and he stayed with the wheat until it had ripened.

"Thank you, droplet, you are very kind!" the wheat said as Dewy left to continue on his journey.

***

Dewy trickled down the wheat stalk, rolled down a slope and found himself in a stream.

"Where are you heading?" he asked the stream.

"I am heading for the fast river, which runs into the mighty ocean," the stream told him.

"Then we are going the same way," Dewy said happily.

"Yes, but there is much work ahead!" the stream warned him.

"Wonderful, I love to help!" Dewy replied.

The stream was whooshing along happily, and the droplets were having fun racing along inside her. But soon Dewy and the other droplets discovered large rocks on their path, making it very difficult for the stream to get through.

"Droplets!" Dewy called out. "Let's clear the way." He began to work quickly with his friends, and together they paved a path for the stream to get through. When the work was done, the stream thanked him saying, "You are a very patient droplet. Thank you."

***

Soon Dewy left the stream and ran into the fast river.

"Where are you heading, fast river?" Dewy asked her.

"I am heading for the mighty ocean," the river answered.

"Then I'll go with you," Dewy said.

He was running along with the river when suddenly they encountered a boat. The boat was also in a hurry to get to the ocean.

"Little droplet, I am in a big hurry," the boat said. Would you push me and make me go faster?" he begged.

Since Dewy was also in a hurry, he knew how much the boat needed his help, and together with his fellow droplets, he carried the boat forward.

"Thank you!" the boat said, speeding away. "You are a very strong droplet."

*** 

The ocean was very close. Dewy could already hear his loud waves. But then a young woman called out to him from the shore: "Oh, droplet, can you help me take care of my little child?"

"Certainly!" Dewy replied and he stayed with the mother and child.

He took care of the child, washed him, played with him, and sang lullabies to him. The child felt very safe and comfortable.

When the time came to say goodbye, both the woman and her child were very thankful.

"Thank you!" they said. "You are a true friend."

*** 

As Dewy did not see anyone else needing his help, he ran to greet the ocean.

"How happy I am to see you again!" the ocean exclaimed, hugging the little droplet.

Dewy was overjoyed. Unable to wait any longer, he asked the question that he had been so eager to know the answer to, "So why do they call you 'mighty'?"

"They call me 'the mighty ocean' because every droplet is very kind, patient, strong, and a true friend to all living things," the ocean said proudly. "I am made of many droplets that are united as one whole. Our strength lies in our unity. Together we form a mighty ocean!"

"Now rest, Dewy," the ocean said, "for you must be tired from your journey."

And a great calmness spread over the ocean.

# A Warm Winter Home

*By Crystlle Medansky*

"Brrr!" whistled Groundhog, poking his head out from under a pile of frosty leaves. "It's s-s-so cold today."

The first frost had sent the last leaves fluttering off the trees, signaling the start of winter.

Groundhog did not like being outside in the cold. "The only place to be in this weather is underground in a warm burrow," he said through chattering teeth.

But Groundhog was hungry for apples. He had been waiting for weeks for the last autumn apples to ripen on the trees. After all, apples are Groundhog's favorite food.

Suddenly, he had an idea.

"I know!" said Groundhog. "First, I will make a warm burrow for the winter. Then, I will come back here to eat the apples."

Leaving footprints in the frost, he left to dig a warm burrow under a hollow tree stump at the edge of the woods.

"I'm s-s-so hungry," he whistled as he dug. "It would be lovely to have s-s-sweet juicy apples."

But all the digging had made Groundhog very sleepy. It was so warm and pleasant inside the burrow that he decided not to go back outside to the apple tree.

Instead, he curled up in the deepest part of the burrow, covering himself with his bushy tail, and went to sleep snoring gently and dreaming of s-s-sweet apples.

Now, Opossum had been searching all morning for a warm shelter and he was about to give up when he spotted the hollow tree stump at the edge of the woods.

"Hurray!" shouted Opossum. "That tree stump will make a perfect shelter for winter."

But there were no leaves near the tree stump to make a fresh bed.

"Hmm," said Opossum, "It would be lovely to have a soft bed. There are still plenty of dry leaves in the woods. I know! I will carry some leaves from the woods with my tail."

So he went back into the woods to fetch dry leaves to make a bed.

Opossum could smell the delicious apple tree on his way back through the woods.

"Yummy, apples!" said Opossum.

Opossum climbed up the tree to pick the last ripe apples, looping them in his tail along with the leaves to carry them to his new shelter.

But Opossum was surprised when he dropped the leaves and apples into the hollow tree stump. The apples rolled one by one down the tunnel into the deepest part of the burrow, waking up Groundhog.

"Who's-s-s there?" whistled a sleepy voice from below.

Opossum curiously peered inside the tree stump.

"Opossum!" said Groundhog poking his head out of the tree stump. "What are you doing at the top of my burrow?"

"Groundhog!" said Opossum. "What are you doing at the bottom of my shelter?"

Groundhog explained that he had spent all morning digging a winter burrow under the hollow tree stump.

Opossum looked very unhappy to hear that.

"What's wrong, Opossum?"

"I spent all morning searching for a warm shelter," sad Opossum sadly. "Then I gathered food and leaves to make a soft bed, and I brought them all here."

Groundhog quickly realized that by uniting, they would have greater strength to survive the cold weather.

"What a wonderful idea!" he whistled, enthusiastically. "After all, I am good at digging, s-s-so it's best that I dug OUR warm burrow. You are good at carrying, s-s-so it's best that you carried OUR s-s-supplies ...And by the way, are those apples I s-s-smell?"

Opossum grinned when he realized what Groundhog meant. Each had contributed something unique to the winter home, and if one part had been missing, it would not be complete.

"Yes," said Opossum, "I brought apples for OUR breakfast!"

So it was that the two friends enjoyed a delicious breakfast of apples and snuggled together for a warm winter nap.

# The Baobab
# that Opened Its Heart

*By Crystlle Medansky*

Long ago, when the big island of Madagascar was but a small village, there lived a young baobab tree. The tropical rains were good for her. Already, she sprouted deep leaves of blue and green.

Then, one midsummer evening, spectacular flowers with soft white petals the size of saucers opened on her stems for the very first time. The fresh petals filled the air with the sweet scent of nectar. The baobab felt as if a beautiful cloud had come down to the ground and wrapped her in sweetness!

"Where is this coming from?" she wondered.

The baobab looked up and smiled when she noticed the clouds in the sky.

"Of course! It's Nature, which gives me the water to grow my beautiful flowers and all the things that make me happy!"

Feeling where her happiness was coming from, the baobab wanted to give something to Nature in return for its kindness.

First, she thought of her deep green leaves, but then she realized that she already received her leaves from Nature. Next, she thought of her beautiful

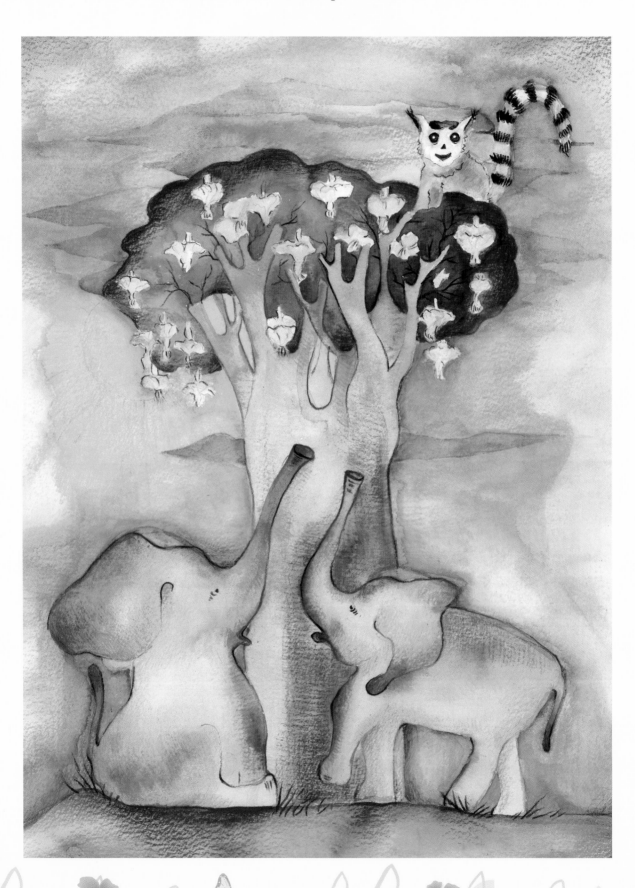

petals, but she also received her petals from Nature. The baobab thought about it for a very long time, but she could not think of anything new she could give to Nature, and this made her feel sad.

But as soon as she felt sad, the breeze blowing past her felt sad, too, and whispered it to the leaves. The leaves whispered it to the birds, and the birds whispered it to the stars. All around her, the baobab could hear her heart whispering: "What can I give to Nature? Must I receive? Is there nothing else?"

Her heart whispered, "I want to give!"

The baobab cried, "I want to be giving like Nature, but I only know how to receive. What am I going to do? Perhaps I should just stop receiving anything!"

Now, Nature had been waiting for exactly this moment; it was time for the baobab to discover her true purpose. That same night, hungry fruit bats swooped down on her flowers to suckle the sweet nectar from her petals. At first, the noisy bats clinging to her petals frightened the baobab.

"My petals, my petals!" she cried, "Why are you ruining my beautiful petals!"

"We are here to carry the pollen to your seed pods," said the bats. "This is how you will grow fruit."

"Ooooh!" cried the Baobab, now understanding. "You are helping me grow fruit! Is the nectar as sweet as it smells?"

"It is delightful; thank you!" replied the bats.

The baobab was happy that the fruit bats had such a tasty dinner. She wasn't even worried when the very next morning all of her beautiful petals fell to the forest floor. She watched happily as the tortoise made a feast of the fallen petals. Now, the baobab felt a sweet new connection to the others nearby.

When the days grew cooler, the baobab began dropping all of her leaves, but the fuzzy fruits remained hanging on her branches. As the tortoise buried himself deep under her leaves to stay warm, the baobab began to wonder how she could give her fruit to Nature. Just then, a troop of lemur monkeys climbed up her branches. Suddenly, there were lemurs everywhere, swinging by their feet to reach the fruits.

"Delicious, delicious!" sang the little lemurs, dangling on her branches.

The baobab giggled with delight, shaking loose her fruit for the hungry little lemurs.

The lemurs leaped between her branches to catch the falling fruit until there were no more left.

With no leaves or fruit at all, the baobab knew her trunk and branches were perfect for storing water. She could give water to the others nearby. During the long season of the dry riverbeds, thirsty elephants tickled her trunk to get a drink. And many other animals squeezed as much water as they needed from her soft, wet bark.

As the seasons passed, the baobab learned how to open a door in her heart to all of Nature's creatures. Her branches with their hollows, dents, and bloated stems became a shelter for bush babies and squirrels, lizards and tree frogs, spiders and snakes. The holes in her trunk became homes for birds and owls.

Nature's plan worked perfectly! The baobab learned how to give. The more she gave, the more she could receive. In this way, she could receive all the happiness that Nature had prepared for her from the beginning.

Now, in the heart of the baobab tree, all Nature's creatures live together in happiness and harmony. And every midsummer evening, she merrily wears a crown of white petals ...because this makes Nature happy, too!

# The Seagull Who Wanted to Be a Turtle

*By Lydia Hora*

One bright summer day, a family of seagulls flew across the sunny sky for a picnic at the beach.

When they arrived, Father Seagull announced, "I will fly over the waves to find fish for our lunch," and he disappeared over the water.

Mother Seagull gathered the flock of seagulls together. "We will practice our flying and collect food that has been left on the beach," she told them. "We can eat it for lunch with the fish that your father will catch."

Happily, the flock of seagulls set off to practice their flying skills, finding scraps of food on the beach and dropping it from high in the sky so they could swoop down and catch it again. But one little seagull was distracted by the waves, and he stopped to look at the ocean. As he watched the waves, he saw a green sea turtle climbing out of the water and onto the soft, sandy beach.

The turtle looked up at the seagull perched on the sand. "Did you fly here?" he asked.

"Yes," answered the seagull. "My family flew here for lunch. I love the beach, but I would rather swim in the ocean. Do you like to swim?"

"I swim all day long, but I wish I could fly like you," the turtle replied. "I love to sit on the beach watching the seagulls fly high in the sky. I wish I could be a seagull."

The seagull looked at the wet green turtle with sand in his toes. "I'd rather be a turtle," he said. "Flying is not that great. I'd much rather swim."

So it was that the green turtle and the young seagull spent the entire morning sharing stories of flying and swimming.

Suddenly, the seagull heard his mother calling him. It was time for lunch. He flew back to his family and enjoyed a delicious lunch of fish and popcorn.

During lunch, the little seagull told his father all about the green turtle. "I wish that I were a turtle so that I could swim all day," he said.

His father looked at him in surprise. "But seagulls fly and clean the scraps that are left on the beach. It's a very important job, you know. Without seagulls, trash would be rotting all over the beach!"

Just then, the seagull family heard someone calling for help. A hermit crab was crawling up and down the beach looking for her son.

"Help! Please help!" she cried. "Please, can you help me find my son? His shell was too small so he set out to look for a larger one. I haven't seen him since this morning when he squeezed out of his old shell."

"My family will be happy to fly over the beach to look for him," replied Father Seagull kindly.

As soon as the little seagull heard this, he flew high up in the sky and began looking for the lost hermit crab.

When the green turtle heard about the lost hermit crab, he wanted to help, too. "Hermit crabs eat sea grass just like me!" he shouted from the water. "I will swim along the shore and search all my favorite rock pools to help you find your son." The friends worked together to find the missing hermit crab. Finally, they found him resting inside his beautiful new shell, and rushed over to greet him.

"My legs were very tired carrying this big shell," said the hermit crab. "I was just looking for a nice, quiet place to rest."

"I could see your big shell sparkling on the clean sand from way up high!" said the seagull.

"You must be hungry!" the turtle exclaimed. "I've been keeping the sea grass short and healthy. Please have some, it's delicious!"

Mother hermit crab was so happy that she scrambled over to her son and hugged him. "Thank you both for helping me find my son!" she said.

The friends were both very happy that they could help.

"Now I understand why it's good to be a seagull," said the young seagull. "Not only can I keep the beach clean, but I can also fly up high to help others."

"And," said the turtle, "Now I understand that it's good to be a turtle, because it's important to keep the sea grass healthy, and I can swim to help others," said the turtle.

At last, the friends had discovered that it's best when each gives to others the thing that makes him special, because this makes everyone happier!

# The Journey of Cocoa Bean

*By Crystlle Medansky*

On the beautiful Ivory Coast, tiny pink petals huddled together on the trunk of a tall tree. Soon, the petals would grow into fruit pods filled with cream-colored beans. Farmers would carefully remove the ripe fruits from the tree and carry them to the edge of the rainforest to dry. The delicate beans inside would be shipped all over the world to make delicious chocolate!

Cocoa was one of these little beans. Each day, she ripened peacefully inside the warm pod with nothing at all to worry about. Cocoa was very happy that soon she would become chocolate—after all, everyone loves chocolate!

But far away, in busy cities everywhere, world leaders were prattling with excitement.

"My fellow countrymen," announced all the leaders. "We have come up with a plan that will bring us all great joy! It has come to our attention that if each country processes cocoa beans for themselves, we will no longer need to rely on each other to make chocolate. This means that we will all have more chocolate for ourselves!"

"Hooray, more chocolate for us!" shouted all the people. "Let's do it!"

Anxious to satisfy their growing appetite for chocolate, workers rushed to build new chocolate factories. Once they got started, more and more people joined them, rushing around in every direction.

The shipyard workers were worried. "If people take more chocolate than they need, there will be no chocolate left for us; instead of building ships, we should be building factories so we can get our share of the chocolate!" they shouted, as they ran to work at the factories.

When the sugar growers heard what was happening, they quickly drove their tractors to the factories to make sure they would get their share of chocolate, too!

Soon, all the people in the world worked from morning until night building more factories to make more chocolate. Giant machines thundered and rolled across the once quiet countryside, and smoke billowed out of towering factories. Sleepy-eyed cows spent all their time grazing in the grassy meadows because there was no one at home to milk them. The once busy shipyards were empty. With each passing day, the factories grew, and so did the little cocoa bean.

"What will become of all these beans without ships to carry them to factories?" asked the cocoa farmer sadly, turning and checking each little bean tenderly. "Everyone is so busy building more factories, they have forgotten about the beans."

When Cocoa Bean heard what the farmer said, she became worried. Already she had developed a rich brown color, a sign that she was ripening. Soon, she would be dry and ready for shipping to the factories.

"If the shipyards stop building and repairing ships, how will we get to the factories?" she asked the other beans.

"Who will build more tractors for the sugar plantations?" she asked. "Everyone knows that you need tractors to plow sugar fields, and to pull the sleds filled with sweet sugar cane to the ships!"

"How will we make chocolate without sugar?" asked another bean.

"And who will milk the cows?" asked Cocoa Bean sadly. "The children love milk chocolate."

"And chocolate ice cream!" chimed the other beans in unity.

Cocoa Bean was very sad. After all, she wanted to bring happiness to others. "How can I bring happiness to others by just lying here in the sun?" she wondered.

Meanwhile, the workers finished the factories.

"Good job, people!" announced the world leaders. "We are ready for business now!"

In a great commotion of cheering and noise, the workers opened the factories and turned on the new machines. All of a sudden, the cheering stopped. The workers realized that they had no beans, sugar, or milk to make the chocolate. Now all the workers began shouting at once.

"We have no beans! We have no sugar! We have no milk! How will we make chocolate?" they cried.

Quickly, they began to blame each other for the mess.

"Why have you not sent us your beans?" the factory workers asked the cocoa farmers angrily.

"The beans are already dried, and ready to pack for shipping. Where are the ships to carry them to the factory?" asked the cocoa farmers.

"And why have you not sent us your sugar?" the workers growled at the sugar growers.

"There is no sugar. We drove our tractors here to build the factories instead of plowing the fields," replied the sugar growers sadly.

"And why have you not sent us your milk?" they asked the dairy farmers.

"We were so busy building the factories that we didn't have any time for milking the cows," replied the dairy farmers.

With no time to lose, the world leaders called a summit.

"Gentlemen," said the leader, "This plan of ours is not working! We have got do something quick! There is no chocolate left in the world! I repeat: THERE IS NO MORE CHOCOLATE!"

"It seems that we must all agree to work together making chocolate," suggested another leader. "Just as Nature gives us exactly what we need to make chocolate, each of us is different and exactly what the others need. If we work together in harmony and take only as much chocolate as we need for ourselves, we will all have enough chocolate."

"Some of us are best at building ships, so we will go back to our shipyards and send ships to carry the beans," offered the shipyard workers.

"We will take our tractors back to the sugar plantations to plow the fields," said the sugar growers.

"Some of us have good land for dairy cows," said another, "so we will go home and milk the cows."

"Let's get going!" they agreed. "We will all work together to make the most delicious chocolate the world has ever seen!"

The great news was sent all around the world. In no time at all, beans, sugar, and milk began arriving at the factories. Liquid chocolate was shipped in tanks and poured into molds for happy confectioners, dairies, and bakeries everywhere. Immediately, the people discovered that by working together in harmony, they not only had enough chocolate, but they also felt a wonderful new connection to one another.

Cocoa Bean was delighted that the people had discovered their mutual responsibility and connection to one another. In fact, she was so happy that when a little boy asked for one scoop of chocolate ice cream, she tickled his tongue until the little boy grinned so widely that his smile barely fit on his face. The little boy's smile filled his mother with pleasure and she smiled, too!

At last, the people of the world learned how to be happy by working together in harmony, just like Mother Nature.

# The Forest May Look Different

*By Meira Levi*

The tall trees in the green forest were moving with the wind. The leaves were playing a soft melody and the sun was rising. Underneath a warm sunbeam, Sammy the Turtle's little head poked out of his armor.

"What a wonderful day," Sammy said to himself, "just like yesterday. I'll go to the fig tree and eat from its sweet leaves."

Every morning, Sammy moved slowly along the purple flowered path until he came to the fig tree. He ate, he slept, and then he went back to his usual place. One morning, Sammy was walking along the purple flowered path. Suddenly, he heard a noise. He turned his head to see a fawn playfully racing toward him. The fawn didn't see Sammy, and before he could put his head inside his armor, he was flying through the air. He tumbled across the grass and landed on the rough ground.

When he stopped, there was silence all around. Even the wind and the melody of the leaves could not be heard. Sammy thought that his eyes were closed, but they were open and he didn't see any light.

"It can't already be evening," he thought.

Sammy didn't recognize where he had landed, so he decided to poke his head out to check where he was. Looking around, he discovered that he had landed in a cave. It was chilly inside the cave but Sammy felt okay. He actually had kind of a homey feeling inside that little cave.

Sammy was hungry. He found a little bush beside him and tasted its leaves. It was very tasty. He saw a scroll that was rolled up and fastened with a lace, hidden in the bushes.

"Wow," said Sammy, "My grandpa once told me about a scroll that was lost many years ago. He said that it had secret writing on it. Could this be the one?"

Sammy pulled the lace and the scroll rolled opened. It was a map. The map led to an enchanted forest with fruit trees, brooks, and spectacular flowers. It was a place where every animal in the world would love to be.

Sammy decided he would find the enchanted forest, come what may. He collected some leaves inside his shell for snacks on the way and started the journey. Sammy walked almost all day long. By evening, he was very tired. He looked back and saw the cave he'd left behind. It was not so far away.

"That's as far as I've gone?" said Sammy, disappointedly. "I am so slow. It may take me another sixty years to reach this wonderful forest."

At that moment, Chuck, the squirrel came hopping down the hill. When he saw Sammy, he stopped his hopping and said, "Hello little turtle; may I help you?"

Sammy told Chuck about the wonderful forest that was drawn on the map that he had found.

"Hey, wow," called Chuck in wonder. "May I join you? I've always dreamed of an enchanted place. I don't know how to read maps, but I am very nimble. I will carry you on my back."

"Wonderful! Great!" called Sammy, and they continued the journey together.

When evening came, Chuck said, "We'll sleep here at the foot of the tree until morning." And they fell asleep immediately.

Morning arrived, the sun was shining and Sammy stuck out his head and called, "Get up Chuck, we should be moving. We've only traveled halfway there."

"My back hurts from carrying you yesterday," said Chuck. "I'll walk slowly with you." They advanced at a turtle's pace, and felt bad that they still had a long way to go. About an hour later, they stopped to have breakfast from a blueberry bush. Tippy, the blue bird, also landed on the bush and started pecking.

"Everything is so tasty," tweeted Tippy. "So why are you sad, Chuck?"

"We have a map to an enchanted, wonderful forest, but it is hard for us to walk fast. It will take us a long time to get there, and we don't want to stay here."

"So..." said Tippy, "How about if I sing to you? That way, the trip will be more pleasant."

"Thank you, thank you very much," said Sammy and Chuck together.

And so the three of them continued on their journey. Sammy read the map and told them which direction to go. Chuck carried Sammy on his back from time to time, and Tippy sang to help make the trip more enjoyable. Every one of them helped the other and together they became a terrific group.

They walked for a few days, maybe a week. They didn't even notice how much time had passed because they had such a wonderful time together. They passed mountains and valleys, fields, and lakes, nights and days. They had such a wonderful time together that they didn't notice that they were walking in a circle....and then it happened.

"We have arrived," called Sammy "It's here, just like it says in the scroll." Sammy tasted the leaves of a green fig tree.

"So tasty! Mmmmm it reminds me a little bit of the tree beside my house, but the taste is... mmmmmm...I've never tasted such sweet leaves as these."

Chuck also started eating from the fruits he picked and said, "Correct, Sammy, the food here is simply delicious, the taste of heaven."

"And the water is so clear," chirped Tippy in her lovely voice.

"One moment," said Sammy, "I think this place is exactly like my home. There's even a path with purple flowers and a fig tree, too." Sammy continued along the path. "And it leads to my house," he called, pointing with his finger toward his house. "I've lived here forever. We walked in a circle and we came back to my house!" called Sammy, and then he burst out laughing. "Now, this forest looks different! Much better than before. In fact, it's wonderful!"

"Right!" twittered Tippy. "I recognize this lake; I drink from it every day, but now the water in it looks bluer."

"Friends, you are definitely right!" said Chuck. "We have always lived here, but every one of us was here separately. But now, being together with such good friends, the house looks joyful and shiny."

"The leaves are crisper," called Sammy.

"The fruits are tastier," said Chuck.

"And the water is sweeter," twittered Tippy.

"This must be the secret scroll," said Sammy, "because it led us to look inside our hearts, and now we see that together, everything becomes wonderful."

"With friends, everything feels great," added Chuck and picked two tasty cherries for Sammy and Tippy.

# The Enchanted Garden

*By Debbie Sirt*

Long ago, there was an enchanted garden. It was the most magnificent place on earth. The sunlight sparked like diamonds as it softly caressed a gentle stream. It reflected the most amazing light that filled the entire garden from beginning to end. The most incredible colors, sweetest fragrances, and lovely sounds were in this garden.

In this wondrous garden lived two children, Benjamin and Eric. They lived together in complete harmony with all the animals, trees, and plants. The children had everything that anyone could ever want and all their days were simply perfect. If they were hungry, all the plants and trees would provide fruits and vegetables for them to eat, and everything tasted wonderful and sweet.

The garden was created especially for the children, to provide them with everything they needed to be happy. But the children did not realize how wonderful their lives were, since they had always lived in the garden and knew only this way of life.

One day, a new tree appeared in the garden. It was an unusual looking tree and it grew a strange-looking fruit. The children were curious, so they decided to investigate. Suddenly a monkey came swinging by on a tree branch, warning the children to be careful.

"Be careful of what?" demanded Benjamin.

"Do not eat this fruit," answered the monkey. "Something bad will ....."

But before the monkey could finish his sentence, Eric picked a fruit off the tree and took a bite.

"Mmmm...this is too delicious to share," said Eric.

"I want some, too," insisted Benjamin as he picked a fruit off the tree and ate it.

Suddenly, a dark cloud covered the garden. At the same moment, the children looked at each other and announced that they no longer wanted to share the garden.

"This will be my side of the garden," said Eric. "You can go and live on the other side."

"That's not fair!" complained Benjamin. "You chose the side with the amazingly sweet fruit!"

The monkey just looked at them and laughed. "You are right. The fruit is amazing, but it's not the taste that makes it amazing. It's the magic inside," the monkey said.

"I want the magic!" exclaimed Benjamin.

"No! I want it!" insisted Eric.

"The fruit has magic seeds inside," the monkey explained. "The seeds reveal your true nature. Now that you ate them, you will only care about yourselves and not about your friend. Look around and see how the garden has changed. You must work together to repair the divided garden, and you must do it with love."

The children looked at the monkey and laughed.

"The only thing better than living in this garden is not sharing it!" Eric exclaimed.

So it was that the children continued to bicker. In fact, the only thing that they agreed about was where to draw a line dividing the garden into two separate places: right down the middle of the amazingly sweet fruit tree!

That night, the children discovered something shocking. All the fruits and vegetables that they ordinarily loved to eat now tasted bitter! Unlike before, the amazingly sweet fruit was the only fruit that still tasted sweet. How could

this be happening? The garden had always taken very good care of them. Both children spit out the bitter fruit and went to bed hungry for the first time.

Benjamin closed his eyes and fell asleep. But Eric stayed awake, worrying about the bitter fruits and vegetables. He decided to gather all the sweet fruits and hide them while Benjamin was sleeping. This way, he would have all of them for himself.

The next morning when Benjamin went to pick a sweet fruit from the tree, he discovered that they were all gone!

"Where did the amazing fruits go?" he thought. "Eric must have taken all of them!"

He looked all over the garden for Eric, but he couldn't find him. Since he was very hungry, he had no choice but to eat some of the bitter fruit. As he bit into the bitter fruit, he got a sharp pain in his side and decided that he would rather go hungry.

Finally, Benjamin was so hungry that he decided to trick Eric into sharing the sweet fruit. He lay down and pretended to be sick. Eric saw his "sick" friend from his hiding place on the other side of the garden and it made him very sad. He walked over to Benjamin and sat next to him.

"You are hungry, right?" he asked Benjamin in a very soft voice.

Benjamin nodded. "I need something to eat, but I can't eat the bitter fruit; it hurts my stomach to eat it," he replied.

Eric realized how selfish he had been, keeping all of the fruits to himself. He suddenly remembered how much fun he used to have playing in the enchanted garden with Benjamin, but now he didn't know if they would ever play together again. Eric's eyes filled with tears, and he quickly ran to his hiding place to bring the sweet fruit to Benjamin.

"Here," he said feeling ashamed. "You can have all the sweet fruits you want. Now I see how selfish I was, keeping them all to myself! The monkey was right, I didn't think about my friend! I would give anything to be back in the enchanted garden with you, the way we used to live."

A look of surprise appeared on Benjamin's face. Now he, too, felt ashamed.

"You may have taken the fruit," he said, "but I tricked you, too... I am not really sick, just hungry. I tricked you into sharing with me! The monkey was right. The fruit did show us our true natures."

"The garden used to take care of us," Eric said. "We had everything we could ever want, but we didn't appreciate it because we were only trying to satisfy ourselves. The magic seeds spoiled everything!"

"Even the sweet fruit!" Benjamin agreed.

Both children stared down at the sweet fruit and discovered that it was starting to rot. Suddenly, Benjamin remembered....

"The monkey said that we must work together to repair the garden!"

"Yes, and we must do it with love!" smiled Eric.

The children decided to work together. Eric squeezed juice out of the sweet fruits and used it to sweeten the bitter fruits and vegetables. It was incredible how it took only a few sprinkles of the juice to add a wonderful flavor to all the other fruits and vegetables! Benjamin planted all of the fruits that had rotted in the ground, and watered them every day.

It wasn't long before the entire garden was filled with an orchard of amazing fruit trees. But fruit trees were not the only thing that grew in the garden; the friendship and love between the children grew so strong that its strength was even more powerful than the magic seeds.

One day, as they were sharing a piece of the amazing fruit together, a miracle had happened: The clouds disappeared from the sky and the sun began to shine again. The children looked up and saw a sky as blue as the ocean. They realized that they were actually back in their beloved garden!

Now, the garden was even better than before, and all the fruits and vegetables were even more delicious. Benjamin stood up and picked a berry. It was the sweetest berry he had ever tasted! All the fruits and vegetables were more delicious than the children could ever have imagined.

From that day on, Eric and Benjamin enjoyed living in the enchanted garden together and eating its fruits. They realized that their friendship was more powerful than the magic seeds. And because of their friendship, the garden would remain perfect forever.

# A Special Treasure

*By Lydia Hora and Marina Fateeva*

In a grove of maple trees at the edge of a shady green forest, there lived three little squirrels named Rusty, Sparky, and Ginger. All winter long the friends snuggled inside the tall tree trunks waiting for spring to arrive. Finally, one morning, a bright sunbeam danced cheerfully among the trees, announcing the first day of spring.

Rusty jumped out of his nest and called to his friends excitedly, "Ginger, Sparky, it's time to go out and play!"

Rubbing the sleep from her eyes, Ginger poked her head out of her nest. "Ooooh," she said with a yawn, "How I missed playing with my friends."

"Hurry up, Ginger!" called Sparky, "Let's run to the forest, and look for juicy berries. I missed summer and strawberries, too!"

Quickly, Ginger leaped from the tree and the three friends scampered off together to find ripe berries. The whole forest was busy. Birds soared through the sky, filling the air with music. The seeds were sprouting, the fruit trees were blossoming, and rain washed the forest in a sea of green leaves.

Soon, summer turned into autumn and the squirrels began searching for nuts and acorns to store for the cold days of winter.

The Baobab that Opened Its Heart

One day, the three squirrels came to a small clearing in the forest. Suddenly Rusty called, "Look, I found a nut! Wow, it's different from any nut that I've seen!"

"That's the BIGGEST nut I ever saw!" Sparky said in amazement. He took the nut and shook it, making a rattling noise. "Such a hard shell!" he said.

"It sounds like there is an ENORMOUS nut inside," agreed Ginger. "I think a nut like this would be very tasty!"

"Let's eat it!" suggested Rusty.

"I don't think that we should eat it," said Sparky. "This nut is special—a real treasure! I don't think there is another nut like this one anywhere in the world."

"Besides, there are three of us, but only one nut," said Ginger thoughtfully. "What shall we do?"

"It's still warm now," said Sparky, "and we have plenty of food. I think we should bury the nut in the ground in case we run out of food during the cold winter. Whoever runs out of food, can come back here to dig up the nut."

All three squirrels agreed this was the best idea, so they buried the nut next to a large hill in the clearing.

Soon winter arrived. One snowy morning, Rusty discovered that he was running out of food. "I know," he thought, "I will go to the clearing and find the nut that we buried." But along the way, Rusty passed his favorite apple tree.

Seeing that there were still a few brown apples withering on the tree, Rusty stopped. "These apples may not taste so good, but I should take them, instead of the nut," he decided. "Perhaps my friends will need the nut more than me."

And with that, Rusty picked the rotting apples and ran back to his warm home inside the tree trunk.

As the cold days of winter continued, the squirrels snuggled deep inside the tree trunks. Then one day, a big wind came and blew across the forest, blowing Ginger right out of her cozy nest! She dusted herself off and looked around in astonishment. The tall maple tree had toppled over and her nest was scattered across the forest. Ginger began gathering up the crumpled branches and twigs to make a new nest, but all of her food was gone. She remembered the nut they had buried and decided to go get it.

On her way to the clearing, Ginger saw a small blueberry bush with some shriveled little berries still clinging to the bare branches. She stopped and thought for a minute: "The nut would probably taste better than these wrinkled old blueberries, but what if Rusty and Sparky do not have any berries left? Perhaps one of them will need the nut more than I do?" And with that, she picked the blueberries and returned to her new home.

Winter was almost over when Sparky decided to take a stroll in the warm sunbeams shining outside his home. At that very moment, a hungry bear that had awakened early from his winter nap passed by Sparky's home. The bear climbed up the tree, taking all the food that Sparky had stored and leaving nothing for Sparky to eat. When the little squirrel returned home, he discovered that all of the food was gone.

At first, Sparky was worried. But then he remembered the nut and ran toward the clearing. He was surprised to find fresh mushrooms growing. "I won't take the nut," thought Sparky. "Perhaps my friends will need it more than me." Instead, he collected the mushrooms and hurried back to his home in the tree.

Spring arrived and then summer, and the three friends decided to check on the nut together. Next to the hill in the clearing, they discovered a great surprise: there was a little tree with lots of nuts growing on it! The squirrels quickly told each other about their winter adventures, how each had decided to save the special nut for his friends. They realized that their friendship had grown stronger, just as the one nut had grown into a tree full of nuts.

Filled with happiness, the friends decided to share this great discovery with the other forest animals. The news quickly spread through the forest. Soon, all of the animals arrived at the clearing to join them. They rested and played together, and shared a delicious feast of nuts.

The squirrels hugged each other and grinned. Finally, they realized that a nut is truly a special treasure because it taught them that love and sharing does far greater good than taking!

# The Harvesters

*By Crystlle Medansky*

The harvesters were tiny little ants. They all looked very much alike, but each ant was different. Some harvesters plucked seeds and some sorted seeds. Some of them dug seed storerooms, and others built the nest.

All summer long, the harvesters harvested seeds. In and out of the nest they marched.

Herbie was one of these little ants. One day, he climbed up a thin blade of grass to pluck the seed, but the plant curled under his weight.

"Humph" said Herbie, back on the ground. "Maybe I could just pluck the seeds from down here."

He squinted and blinked but he could not see any seeds at the bottom of the plant. Herbie moved from plant to plant looking for seeds until he heard the other ants gathering to march back to the nest.

"Oh no," said Herbie, "I didn't find any seeds."

"Don't worry, Herbie! Come on! You can help carry these seeds back to the nest," said another ant as he scurried past.

When Herbie saw all the ants waiting for him, he hurried to join them.

Back at the nest, Herbie decided to try sorting seeds.

"Good harvest today! Lots of seeds!" said the other ants.

"Oh, umm yes, I see," said Herbie. But really, Herbie could not see; the seeds were very small and he was having a hard time sorting them.

"Maybe I need to have my eyes checked," said Herbie. "I mean, these seeds are very small ...I think I may be seeing double!"

"Herbie, my friend," suggested another ant, "maybe you could try digging or building." He continued, "There's no need to worry, there is plenty that you can do to help."

"Thanks! Good idea," said Herbie, eagerly. "I will try digging!"

Herbie followed the tunnel into the nest. Many harvesters were working together in the tunnel. Some were digging and others were passing clumps of dirt from ant to ant.

Herbie quickly found a spot next to a digger. The digger was scooping out dirt enthusiastically and a huge mound of dirt was piling up beside him.

"Hey, I haven't seen you here before," said the digger.

"This is my first day digging!" said Herbie, excitedly.

"There's nothing to it, my friend," said the digger. "You just scoop out the dirt and move it aside, and then you scoop it and move it again. It's good exercise! Just let me know if you need any help."

Herbie tried to dig, but the dirt was very hard. Suddenly, a clump of dirt broke loose, covering Herbie. "Mmm, yes, I see what you mean," said Herbie, coughing and brushing himself off.

"Why don't you try passing the dirt out of the tunnel?" asked the digger.

Herbie was disappointed. "I think maybe I will just go outside and get some fresh air first," he said, sadly.

Outside, Herbie saw harvesters carrying pebbles and grass cuttings to build the nest.

"Finally, this looks like something important that I could do to help!" said Herbie, and he rushed to join them.

Herbie stepped in line to take a pebble, but it was very heavy and he collapsed under the weight.

"Easy there," said another ant, lifting the pebble off Herbie. "Why don't you carry a blade of grass? Just hang on tight so it doesn't blow away."

Herbie took a blade of grass. As he began to march to the nest, the wind blew and Herbie lost it. He started to run after the blade of grass, but it floated away on the breeze.

"Let it go. It happens to everyone," called another ant. "You'll get it next time."

"Ugh!" moaned Herbie, "I can't even carry a little blade of grass!"

Discouraged, Herbie stopped trying to pluck, sort, dig, or build. He just hung around the nest watching all the other harvesters scurry around him.

"It's not right," he mumbled to himself. "There must be something important that I can do."

Finally, for the first time, Herbie left the nest by himself. He marched out of the colony and right off the path!

Standing alone in the meadow, Herbie's eyes widened at the size of everything. The grass was so tall he couldn't reach the top, even on his tiptoes. Prickly pokeweeds made giant shadows on the ground. Big insects buzzed all around him. Suddenly, Herbie felt very small.

He felt a little better when he spotted another harvester. But when Herbie got closer, he saw that it was not a harvester after all. It was a spider.

"WOW!" said Herbie. "You must be very strong. I bet that you can pluck, sort, dig, and build faster than any harvester."

"Of course!" said the spider.

"Maybe I could stay and help you," said Herbie.

"Help me? How could a tiny little ant help me?" asked the spider.

Before Herbie could think of an answer, he heard his name. "Herbie?" someone called to him.

The voice was familiar. Herbie turned around to see another harvester.

"Herbie! How happy I am to see you! We have been looking everywhere for you. Come and let me have a look at you. Hmmm," said the harvester as he looked at Herbie, "Looks like you are still in one piece. We were worried about you."

"I didn't mean to worry you," said Herbie. "I really tried to pluck and sort. I tried my best to dig and build."

"Oh, you don't have to explain, Herbie. We all know how hard you worked."

"You do?" asked Herbie, surprised.

"Of course!" said the harvester. "It's not important how much work each ant can do alone; what's important is that we work together! When we work together, every ant feels the strength of the whole group."

Happily, Herbie marched right back on the path!

He followed the tunnel into the nest and quickly found a spot next to a digger.

"Hey, you came back!" said the digger.

"Yes," smiled Herbie, "And I am feeling much stronger now!"

# Warmly Suggested

### The Wise Heart;
### Tales and allegories of three contemporary sages

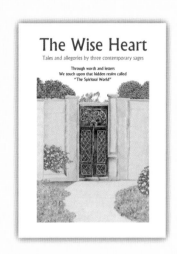

*The Wise Heart* introduces a lovingly crafted anthology of tales and allegories by Kabbalist Dr. Michael Laitman, his mentor, Rav Baruch Ashlag (Rabash), and Rabash's father and mentor, Rav Yehuda Ashlag, author of the *Sulam* (Ladder) commentary on *The Book of Zohar*. The allegories herein provide a glimpse into the way Kabbalists experience the spiritual world, with surprising, and often amusing depictions of human nature, with a tender touch that is truly unique to Kabbalists.

### Together Forever: the story about the magician who didn't want to be alone

In *Together Forever*, the author tells us that if we are patient and endure the trials we encounter along our life's path, we will become stronger, braver, and wiser. Instead of growing weaker, we will learn to create our own magic and our own wonders as only a magician can. In this warm, tender tale, Michael Laitman shares with children and parents alike some of the gems and charms of the spiritual world. The wisdom of Kabbalah is filled with spellbinding stories. *Together Forever* is yet another gift from this ageless source of wisdom, whose lessons make our lives richer, easier, and far more fulfilling

### Miracles Can Happen
### (tales for children, but not only...)

For children of all ages: ten enchanting tales that describe how *Miracles Can Happen* when we open our eyes to the joy and beauty that comes from being connected with others. This heartfelt collection of children's stories creates an appreciation for Nature's wondrous ways, revealing the eternal truth that only together can we do something truly wonderful.

# HOW TO CONTACT
# BNEI BARUCH

1057 Steeles Avenue West, Suite 532
Toronto, ON, M2R 3X1
Canada

Bnei Baruch USA,
2009 85th street, #51,
Brooklyn, New York, 11214
USA

E-mail: info@kabbalah.info
Web site: www.kabbalah.info

Toll free in USA and Canada:
1-866-LAITMAN

Fax: 1-905 886 9697